The Grumpy Guidebook

2024 Holiday Edition

The Grumpy Guidebook

A Step-By-Step Guide Through the Transition from Middle-Aged and Successful to Old and Grumpy

Old & Grumpy, LLC
Vincent Fratto and Michael Fayol

Copyright © 2024 Old & Grumpy, LLC
Written by: Vincent Fratto & Michael Fayol
Illustrated by: Ian Chamberlin
Edited by: Marni MacRae

All rights reserved.
ISBN: 9798343323573

Contents

Volume 1: Grumpy Expressions

Volume 1 Prologue 6

Chapter 01.
The Art of Grumpy Facial Expressions 8

Chapter 02.
The Grumpy Sigh - Exhaling Dissatisfaction 18

Chapter 03.
The Art of Grumpy Commentary - Verbal Volleys of Wit 28

Continuing Education in Grumpiness 42

Volume 2: Grumpy Pastimes

Volume 2 Prologue 46

Chapter 01.
Grumpy Hobbies – Around the House 48

Chapter 02.
Grumpy Physical Pursuits 64

Chapter 03.
Grumpy Adventures - Embracing Discontented Explorations 81

Signing off with a sigh 96

About The Authors 97

Volume 1 Prologue

Welcome you, my fellow curmudgeon, to the start of your transition, your journey from middle-aged and successful to old and grumpy, and you, sir, deserve a hearty congratulations! You have spent a lifetime in traffic, in a cubical or retail store, a restaurant or service garage, and have piled up professional success after success and failure after failure (for what is success with no failure to compare it to?). Whatever your path, you have done it, all your years of dealing with other people's b.s. has led to this inevitable statement—you're old now and let's face it, kind of grumpy.

Don't recoil from that statement, be proud, you should be! Here you find yourself on the precipice of grumpy greatness, like the elders that have come before you. But you are new here and unsure of yourself, anxious about how to proceed with this natural next step in your age evolution. Here lies before you the eternal question; How do I hone my grumpy skills for the next chapter of my life to make my grumpy years as successful as my professional years?

Have no fear, my grumpy grasshopper, I will lead you through the illuminating journey of becoming a grumpy old man! I will walk you through in great specificity and detail how to master all aspects of grumpy greatness so that when your time on this crazy blue marble is done, others will think of you, saying, "Boy, he sure was grumpy," and what more can a man ask for in a legacy?!

In our first chapter, we shall embark on an enlightening adventure, exploring the subtle art of grumpy facial expressions. So, gather your furrowed brows and prepare to perfect that world-class scowl!

VOLUME 1
GRUMPY EXPRESSIONS

CHAPTER 1:
The Art of Grumpy Facial Expressions

Mastering the Eyebrow Raise

Ah, the eyebrow raise. An indispensable tool in the arsenal of any self-respecting grump. With just a subtle lift of the brow, we can convey a multitude of emotions without uttering a single word. It is the silent language of disapproval, the universal signal of disdain, and our secret weapon in the battle against cheerful exuberance.

Now, you might wonder, why should we bother perfecting this particular maneuver? Well, my friend, the answer lies in the sheer satisfaction of watching others squirm under the weight of our withering gaze. It's the unspoken power that accompanies a perfectly executed eyebrow raise, leaving unsuspecting souls questioning their life choices, their fashion sense, and, if done correctly, their very existence.

But fear not, for I shall guide you through the intricacies of this grumpy art form. First, find yourself a mirror, for self-reflection is the cornerstone of our journey. Stand before it, brow furrowed, face set in a determined scowl, and let us begin.

The Foundation

To commence our training, let's start with the basics. Relax your facial muscles and take a deep breath, take a second, and think back to your last trip to the supermarket and a random fool you had to suffer through. Any commonplace idiot will do, like that Grade A moron in the produce section weighing one organic avocado vs the other in exaggerated up and down arm motions like it actually makes a difference. He's perfect, keep him in mind. Now, with that food for thought, raise one eyebrow slowly, as if effortlessly challenging the world to meet your unimpressed gaze. Hold it there for a moment, keep it steady, good, allow the dissatisfaction to seep into your very being. Excellent, well done! Repeat this exercise with the other brow, ensuring both eyebrows receive equal attention. It's important not to form a dominant brow (be it left or right), that will throw off the formation of your forehead wrinkles, and no one wants that.

Mastering the Subtleties

Remember, my grumpy apprentice, subtlety is key, for in the realm of grumpy expressions, less is often more. The true master of subtleties understands the power of restraint and the art of the slight raise, that fractional lift that conveys volumes without overt effort. It is in the delicate balance between minimal movement and profound impact that the essence of grumpy expressions lie. Practice in front of your mirror with diligence, honing your ability to execute these subtle gestures with precision. Keep your movements measured and controlled, like a salty maestro conducting an orchestra of grumpy emotions. Just as a skilled conductor guides each section of the orchestra to create a harmonious symphony, so too must you orchestrate a captivating performance of agitation and discontent.

Well done, always remember; through the gentle elevation of an eyebrow, you can communicate skepticism, silently questioning the absurdity that surrounds you. With a barely perceptible narrowing of your eyes, you cast a shadow of suspicion upon those fools who dare to cross your grumpy path. These nuanced movements, when executed with the right amount of finesse, serve as the brushstrokes that paint a vivid portrait of your inner turmoil and discontentment.

Don't go overboard here, it is not the grand theatrics that define a true grumpy master but the subtle and controlled expressions that leave others unsettled with the folly of their ways. It is the unspoken language of your beautifully grumpy soul, capable of conveying more than a thousand words ever could. That is the true essence of the subtle brow raise.

Advanced Variations

Now that you have grasped the fundamentals, let us embark on a journey through the advanced spectrum of emotions your eyebrow raise can masterfully convey. Prepare yourself for an exploration of grumpy expressions that will elevate your eyebrow game to new heights. Let's take a moment here to stretch your face—we aren't spring chickens anymore, and the last thing we want is a trip to the ER with a world-class face cramp. While that might help your overall grump level, it's not worth it.

Okay, all stretched and loose, now we are ready for some advanced level brow movements.

Exploring beyond the realm of the ordinary, brace yourself for the epic unveiling of "The Browlift Cataclysm." This look is honed through countless hours of eye-rolling at the follies of humanity. This look requires raising both brows in perfect unison with a stone-cold stern expression glued to your face, your mouth perfectly parallel to your raising brows. As your brows ascend as one, the world around you becomes the recipient of your delicate yet demonstrative admonishment, for its

> **PRO TIP:**
>
> *add a slight smirk at the same time to really drive it home. Angle your smirk to the same side as the raised brow*

lack of sophistication is unworthy of your admiration. This expression exudes an aura of refined indifference, silently proclaiming your disapproval and disdain with resounding clarity.

Next, take a moment to look around you to ensure your surroundings are safe and secure before we move on to "The Sarcastic Arch of Condemnation," a grandiose spectacle that transcends mere eyebrow raises. For this execution, focus only on a single brow and rapidly ascend it, not in a mere display of disdain but in a sardonic dance of mockery. This audacious maneuver showcases your unparalleled wit and keen awareness of the absurdities that engulf us all. As your brow ascends, add a dash subtle smirk, strictly on the same side as the raised brow, which will incite a ripple of disbelief reverberating through onlookers like a shockwave, casting doubt upon their own rationality and questioning the very essence of their taste. "The Sarcastic Arch of Condemnation" is a tour de force, a theatrical masterpiece that intertwines grumpy prowess with the art of subtle mockery. It is an expression that demands attention, a gesture that serves as a wake-up call to the delusions of society. With this singular movement, you become the curator of wit, the maestro of irony, and the herald of truth. Embrace the power it bestows upon you and revel in the bewilderment of those who are privileged enough to witness this remarkable feat of your artisanal mastery of grump.

Finally, behold as we unveil the captivating marvel known as "The Summit of Elevated Scorn," a technique that demands unwavering precision, finesse, and undivided attention. This extraordinary expression is reserved for the elite grumpy connoisseurs and requires precise control over each muscle fiber involved in the elevation of a single brow. Pay attention to the angle now, ensure it is sharp yet refined, project a profound sense of confident authority. Allow the situation to dictate the speed of said raise. Practice maintaining a relaxed facial expression throughout while focusing solely on the movement of your eyebrow. As your brow powerfully ascends, it serves as a lofty proclamation, an insignia of your elevated status above the mundane and extraordinarily ridiculous alike. In that fleeting moment, you become the epitome of discerning judgment, casting your critical gaze upon the world with a regal air.

When done right, "The Summit of Elevated Scorn" transcends the realm of man, exuding an air of Mount Olympus-level of superiority that leaves no room for doubt. With impeccable control, a dash of panache, and the might of Zeus himself, you declare your intellectual prowess, positioning yourself as a distinguished Lord of Refined Grumpiness who is second to none.

You are now at the pinnacle of grumpy expressions, an artform mastered by us chosen few who possess the audacity to stand above the fray. With this singular gesture, you navigate the heights of refined grumpiness, surveying the lesser beings from your lofty perch as your face screams out 'begone, vile mortals!'

That was tough, but we made it through to the other side! Pat yourself on the back, this is really advanced-level stuff we are dealing with here. Take a breath and get a drink if you need before we move on.

Grumpy Expressions

Fine-Tuning and Personalization

Well done, my grumpy brother, we have arrived at a pivotal moment in your journey toward grumpy enlightenment. This is where the true artistry of the grumpy expression unfolds—the realm of fine-tuning and personalization. As with any art form, the eyebrow raise is an expression of your individuality, a canvas upon which you leave your distinct grumpy fingerprint. Now is the time to embrace your unique style, to experiment with your own variations, and to refine your grumpy persona.

No two grumpy individuals are alike, and each of you possesses a singular essence that sets you apart from the rest. As you embark on the exploration of eyebrow raises, let your creativity flourish—just have fun with it! Experiment with angles, intensities, and speeds, and observe how each subtle adjustment transforms the message conveyed by your lifted brow. Beware though, a little goes a long way here. Add a little too much flair to "The Browlift Cataclysm," for example, and empires fall. This look was the true reason Rome fell, so use it well but beware of its power.

Take inspiration from the grumpy greats who have come before you, but do not be confined by their styles. Instead, infuse their wisdom with your personal touch, combining their techniques with your own idiosyncrasies. In doing so, you will cultivate a style that is entirely yours—one that carries the weight of your grumpy experiences and the depths of your discernment. As you embark on your journey of fine-tuning and personalization, remember that grumpiness is an ever-evolving art. Embrace the joy of exploration, the delight in discovering new expressions that perfectly encapsulate your exasperation. Allow your grumpy persona to grow, to adapt, and to surprise even yourself.

And so, gentlemen, let us forge ahead with unwavering determination. Hone your eyebrow raises, seek out the subtleties that resonate with your soul, and sculpt your grumpy identity with purpose and conviction. In this realm of personalization, you have the power to create a legacy—a legacy of grumpiness that reflects the true essence of who you are.

In Conclusion

Congratulations, my fellow grump-in-the-making! You have taken your first steps toward becoming a master of grumpy facial expressions. Through dedicated practice and a commitment to embracing your inner curmudgeon, you will forge a path to grumpy enlightenment, a course paved with scowls and raised eyebrows. As you continue your journey, remember that grumpiness is a talent that evolves with age. With each passing day, you will discover new depths of grumpiness within you, polishing your skills and perfecting your expressions is a key part of the transition from middle aged and successful to old and grumpy.

Let us not forget that grumpiness is not an end in itself. It is a means to an end, a tool to navigate the trials and tribulations of life with a touch of humor and a dash of irreverence. It is a reminder to never take ourselves too seriously, to find joy in the absurdity of the world around us.

So, my grumpy comrade, as we conclude this introductory chapter, let us raise our eyebrows in unison, basking in the collective grumpiness that binds us together. May your scowls grow deeper, your eye-rolls sharper, and your wit be honed to a sharp edge. And always remember, a well-executed grumpy expression is worth a thousand words.

In the next chapter, we shall delve into the art of perfecting the grumpy sigh, a cornerstone of our repertoire. Prepare yourselves, for a world of exasperation awaits. Until then, my fellow grump, embrace your crotchetiness and wear it proudly. Onward we march, toward a future filled with wrinkled brows and witty retorts!

CHAPTER 2:
The Grumpy Sigh – Exhaling Dissatisfaction

The Grumpy Sigh - Exhaling Dissatisfaction

With the mastery of the Grumpy Facial Expressions in our back pocket, let us now gather around and immerse ourselves in the captivating realm of the grumpy sigh. In the following pages, you discover how to employ a symphony of frustration, a sonata of annoyance, giving testament to the weariness that resides deep within our grumpy souls. In this chapter, we shall embark on a profound journey, unravelling the intricate components that give birth to the grumpy sigh and exploring the vast emotions it embodies. Brace yourself, my comrade, for we are about to embark on a harmonic expedition that will resonate with the very essence of our grumpiness.

The grumpy sigh is not a mere exhale of air but a profound expression of our exasperation, a release of pent-up frustration that resonates through our being. It carries the weight of countless annoyances and grievances, drawing upon a lifetime of encounters with the irritating aspects of the world.

To truly master the art of the grumpy sigh, we must first understand its intricate components. The grumpy sigh is a language of its own, spoken by countless grumpy souls throughout the ages. It is a language that transcends words, an ancient dialect understood by our fellow grumps. With each sigh, we communicate our shared frustration, our weariness with the world's absurdities, and our longing for a simpler, more sensible existence. It is a sigh that echoes the sentiments of grumpy minds across generations, binding us together in a harmonious chorus of discontent.

Grumpy Expressions

So, my grumpy brother, let us embrace the grumpy sigh in all its glory as we explore its nuances, practice its cadence, and unleash its power upon the world.

Step 1: The Breath of Exasperation

A grumpy sigh is not merely a casual exhalation; it is a deliberate and purposeful act of releasing pent-up frustration upon a simpleton in your presence. To truly master the art of the grumpy sigh, we must begin with the breath—the foundation upon which our discontentment rests.

Close your eyes and take a deep breath, pull again from a random fool as food for your grumpiness. Now, inhale slowly, allowing the air to fill your lungs with the weight of the world's follies. Feel the heaviness settle upon your shoulders, an invisible burden that only we, the grumpy few, carry. As you breathe in, let the essence of your grumpiness permeate every fiber of your being. Absorb the countless irritations, the nonsensical behaviors, and the ludicrous inconveniences that surround us. Allow them to merge and mingle with your inner grump, creating a concentrated swirling vortex of exasperation within you (pro tip: This is not a passive inhalation but an active absorption of all that fuels your grumpy soul).

Good, very good. Now, as you reach the peak of inhalation, hold that breath for a brief moment, savoring the anticipation of what is to come. The air within you is now charged with the energy of grumpiness, ready to be unleashed. The breath of exasperation sets the stage for the grand performance of your grumpy sigh, the masterful release of discontent.

Step 2: The Release of Discontent

Now comes the climactic moment of truth—the release of our discontent. With a deliberate exhalation (and let's be honest; a bit of a flair for the dramatic) that seems to stretch on for an eternity, let out a sigh that speaks volumes of your discontent. It should be a sigh so profound, so magnificently elongated, that it transcends the boundaries of trivial matters such as 'time and space' and becomes the embodiment of your weariness, irritation, and resignation upon the sigh's recipient.

The sound should resonate through the air, as if the universe itself pauses to listen to your grumpy proclamation. Let it be a sigh that encapsulates the collective frustration of grumpy souls across eons. A sigh so deep and lengthy that it surpasses the mere limitations of human understanding. Allow it to stretch out, like a lazy cat luxuriating in the warmth of a sunbeam. You know you are doing it right when the sigh meanders through the air, weaving its way into the consciousness of all who have the privilege of hearing it!

Expressive Variations

Like a grumpy maestro, you have the power to imbue your sigh with different emotions and meanings. Let us explore some expressive variations to elevate your grumpy sigh's game.

The "Heavyweight Sigh"

HEAVYWEIGHT SIGH

Picture yourself carrying the weight of the world on your shoulders, because, in all honesty, this is our duty as a grump. Once you have the entire earth fixed upon your back, let out a sigh that conveys the burden of your existence, making others acutely aware of the struggles that accompany your grumpy wisdom—whether they asked for it or not. As the Heavyweight Sigh escapes your lips, it fills the space around you with a thick, tangible presence. It hangs in the air, enveloping those nearby in its aura of grumpy authenticity. The sound should be deep and resonant, conveying the weight of your existence with each passing second. It should echo through the room, a solemn reminder of the battles fought and the scars earned. The Heavyweight Sigh can be enjoyed in a group of others, say at a family gathering or a movie theater, or by yourself in a street café or walking around in your town's square. Sometimes it's nice simply to let out a Heavyweight sigh even when alone, unprovoked. It has a satisfying melody that sooths the soul upon release.

The "Utter Disbelief Sigh"

DISBELIEF SIGH

Encounter an act of sheer stupidity? Exhale a sigh that communicates your utter disbelief at the lack of common sense and elegance in the world. Through this combined gesture, you assert your place as a grumpy sage, witnessing the absurdities of the world with a critical eye and unapologetic candor. It is a reminder that you are old, dammit, and expressing your disdain for the lack of class you see before you is your privileged duty.

PRO TIP:
combine this with an eyeroll for maximum effect and efficiency.

Grumpy Expressions

The "Pitying Sigh"

PITYING SIGH

Witness someone making foolish choices? Let out a sigh that carries an undertone of pity, as if silently acknowledging their impending regret. This sigh speaks volumes without uttering a single word. Imagine the scene unfolding before your eyes—a person confidently embarking on a path of folly, oblivious to the consequences that lie ahead. It could be a friend making ill-advised financial decisions or a colleague pursuing a doomed romantic entanglement. Regardless of the specific ridiculous circumstance, your grumpy wisdom allows you to see the inevitable outcome with utmost clarity, and it is your duty as resident grumpy old man to express it with a Pitying Sigh. This sigh serves as a non-verbal cue, inviting the person to reconsider their choices and potentially course-correct before it's too late. It acts as a silent guardian, offering a gentle nudge toward the path of wisdom that you can clearly see before them.

Timing and Delivery

Timing is everything when it comes to the grumpy sigh. It must be executed with impeccable precision to maximize its impact. Choose your moments wisely, my grumpy disciple. Let the sigh escape just as someone utters a particularly ridiculous statement or when faced with yet another mind-numbing inconvenience from yet another fool. Now is your time to strike!

Remember, the grumpy sigh is not a one-size-fits-all solution. It should be meticulously crafted and tailored to fit each unique situation, each exasperating annoyance, and each unfortunate person who has the misfortune of crossing your grumpy path. In the grand tapestry of grumpiness, your sigh becomes a personalized brushstroke, painting a vivid picture of your discontent and dissatisfaction with others. Always consider the individuals on the receiving end of the sigh as well. Are they oblivious souls who require a sigh dripping with sarcasm and biting irony? Or are they more receptive to a sigh tinged with a touch of empathy and understanding? Tailor your grumpy sigh to elicit the desired response—a momentary pause, a pang of guilt, or a glimmer of self-awareness. Remember, you are the grumpy elder statesman, the sigh recipient will look to you for your grumpy guidance and direction, so don't be shy to give it to them in spades.

Advancing your Grumpy sigh

The grumpy sigh might be a simple two-step process, but as any discerning grumpster knows, the journey to perfection is an unyielding one. There are still greater heights to be attained, and the grumpy sigh is all about a strong finish so you can bask in your sigh's glory. This is where you infuse your sigh with an aura of pure grumpy brilliance to take it to a whole new level. In this advanced stage, your sighs become more than just exhalations of discontent; they become masterpieces of grumpiness that leave an indelible mark on all who encounter them.

Let's explore a few tried and true finishing moves. This is by no means a complete list but rather a few highlights for you to get your grumpy juices flowing.

The Echoing Resonance

Unleash the power of your grumpy sighs by creating an echoing resonance that reverberates through the corridors of frustration. As you release your sigh, allow it to bounce off the walls of indifference, amplifying its impact and making your discontent heard far and wide. Let the echoes of your sigh linger in the air, serving as a haunting reminder of your grumpy presence and leaving a lasting impression on those within earshot.

The Sigh-Fueled Rant

Elevate your grumpy sighs to new heights by transforming them into powerful fuel for a grumpy rant. After exhaling your sigh of discontent, let the words flow with precision and eloquence, delivering a scathing commentary on the absurdities of life. This well-orchestrated blend of sighs and speech will leave your audience astounded by your grumpy eloquence.

The Sigh Signature

Just as a painter signs their masterpiece, so too must you leave your mark on the world with your signature grumpy sigh. Develop a unique sigh that becomes your calling card, a sigh so distinctive that it is recognized as yours alone. Let your sigh serve as a badge of honor, declaring your status as a true artisan of grumpiness.

CHAPTER 3:
The Art of Grumpy Commentary – Verbal Volleys of Wit

Before we embark on this journey, it is my responsibility to give a word of caution: the realm of grumpy commentary holds an intoxicating power that few can resist. We must proceed carefully into this domain, where a captivating warning prevails. Brace yourself, for within this chapter lies the instructions for you to become a true artisan of grumpy commentary and witty banter.

Let us venture together now, you and I, into this enchanting world where the art of crafting witty verbal volleys takes center stage. Here, your words will become the tool of your grumpy expression, allowing you to convey your dissatisfaction with unrivaled precision. Prepare to unleash your linguistic prowess and engage in the delightful dance of grumpy banter so your growing grumpiness is not only felt and seen but heard.

You must understand that the true power of grumpy commentary lies not only in the words we choose but also in the way we deliver them. As with Grumpy Facial Expressions and Grumpy Sighs, timing is crucial, for a well-timed quip can land with devastating effect, leaving our targets speechless and our fellow grumps in awe of our command of grumpy wit.

Follow my lead, and I will help you to refine your linguistic skills, sharpening your tongue and linguistic dexterity to become a true master of grumpy wit. Now we take our first steps into the realm of subtle wordplay, embracing puns, double entendres, and clever phrasing to inject a touch of grumpy whimsy into our everyday conversation.

Grumpy Expressions

Grumpy Commentary in Everyday Life

Incorporate grumpy commentary into your everyday exchanges, transforming mundane conversations into moments of grumpy delight. Inject yourself, forcefully if you must, into foolish and questionable opinions with carefully crafted remarks that leave no doubt about your grumpy stance. Wasn't there at the start of the conversation? Not sure exactly what the conversation is about? Who cares? Inject anyway, it's your grumpy right!

Remember, the goal is not to foster positive change or win people over, that time has passed. Your aim is to assert your grumpy presence and make yourself heard in every conversation. Let your words carry the weight of your grumpy disposition. They have the power to shape the narrative and leave a lasting impression that will reverberate long after the conversation is over.

Grumpy commentary is not confined to formal settings or structured conversations; it has the power to permeate the very fabric of your everyday life, becoming an integral part of your grumpy persona. Take the opportunity in every interaction to unleash your grumpy wit and make your voice heard. Practice at home as often as possible—just don't ruffle your significant other, you'd be on your own, I can't help you there. This book is about successfully navigating the transition to becoming grumpy, not navigating the impossible. Hey... actually, if you're writing a book on that subject, or know of one, send it my way. I can certainly use the help in that regard!

The Elements of Grumpy Commentary

Grumpy commentary is more than a mere exchange of words. It is an intricate dance, a ballet of sharp wit and acerbic humor. To master this art, we must first understand its fundamental elements.

The 1st Element: Timing and Delivery

Ah, timing and delivery—the twin pillars upon which grumpy conversations are built. Let's practice now; imagine yourself in a conversation, your grumpy senses tingling with anticipation—now is the time to strike. Let the words linger in the air to build suspense like a magician holding the final card. Then, with the precision of a skilled surgeon, unleash your grumpy remark. It should hit its target with the force of a grumpy thunderbolt, leaving your audience hanging on the edge of their seats, yearning for more grumpy brilliance.

Timing is the secret ingredient that separates the amateurs from the true grumpy masters. It's like delivering the perfect punchline, but instead of laughter, you aim for a chorus of grumpy acknowledgment. So, be patient, savor the moment, it's important not to rush it. When you unleash your grumpy charm at just the right instant and strike with impeccable timing, the impact will be nothing short of grumpy magic.

Don't forget to stick your delivery as well; it's equally important. Your tone of voice should reflect the very essence of your grumpiness. Picture it as a blend of weary resignation, subtle irritation, and a pinch of dry sarcasm. Let your words drip with the weight of your discontentment, delivered with a deadpan expression that adds an extra layer of grumpy charm. Remember, it's not just what you say but how you say it that amplifies the impact of your grumpy commentary. Pro tip: Mix in advanced facial expressions or start with a grumpy sigh to really separate yourself.

The 2nd Element: Satire and Irony

Now we get to the real meat and potatoes of Grumpy Conversation, where satire and irony reign supreme. Stand before your trusty mirror again... what do you mean you're not at your mirror. Okay, I'll give you a minute to walk there. Geez, don't let me keep you... okay, good (wow, you walk slowly). Right, let's jump back into this. You took too long, and I lost my place. Where were we? Ah, right! Timing and Delivery! Wait, hold on, I think we already did that. Satire and irony, that's it! Next time try to be prepared. Okay. Satire and Irony. Prepare to unlock the full potential of your grumpy wit.

The Art of Grumpy Commentary - Verbal Volleys of Wit

Mastering the art of delivering biting remarks that will leave others both belittled and enlightened. This is not a casual endeavor, mind you—it requires dedication and finesse. You've gotten this far into this book, so you're certainly dedicated, I'll give you that; finesse, though, well, that still remains to be seen, but I believe in you.

So, gaze at your reflection, summoning the spirit of sarcasm that lies within. Craft your words with precision, stripping away the mask of societal absurdities to expose the contradictions and follies that surround us. Now, with a mischievous glint in your eye, let your words dance with playful venom. Deliver your remarks with impeccable timing and a tone that brims with ironic amusement. Observe how your reflection reacts, and let it be your guide. As you stand there, in front of your mirror, explore the delightful tension between what is said and what is meant; how the subtle nuances of your delivery make the words come alive with their intended and unintended meaning alike.

> **PRO TIP:**
> *A simple "yeah" or "Yup" delivered just right is worth more than any sentence.*

With each practice session, refine your artistry. Fondly embrace the duality of satire and irony and become a master of wielding their power. Trust your judgement here, and once you feel you are ready, step out into the world, armed with your newfound skills, and let your grumpy brilliance shine and the world quake beneath your grumpy feet.

The 3rd Element: Observational Grumpiness

As you continue to stand before your mirror, my seasoned grump, let us take a closer look at observational grumpiness. Here we will work on training your senses and cultivating a keen eye for the irritants that surround us in this ever-changing world. This is not a mere exercise in observation but a defiant stand against the ways of the younger generations... pfft, damn kids.

I can give you the building blocks here, and we can make observations about how dirty that mirror is or how the toilet paper roll was inserted upside down, but the true forum of observation lies out in the world populated with everyday fools. You can take the lessons you learn here to train yourself to spot the idiosyncrasies and quirks that others overlook. The things that really grate on your seasoned grumpy soul, like new modern trends and unneeded technologies that just complicate things, crazy styles and that god forsaken new 'music.' The outside world is literally filled like an endless sea with ridiculousness just waiting to be plucked off the giving tree.

Look for opportunities to expose and express your grumpy frustrations, injecting them into the flow of dialogue with a touch of seasoned wisdom. Your observations of these irritants will naturally seep into your conversations like a relentless drumbeat. It could be a disdainful comment about the reliance on smartphones or a simple remark about the superiority of "our" music. Whatever the observation, it's a dish best served cold with a comparative side dish consisting of "the way it used to be was better."

By seamlessly integrating your grumpy observations, you transform everyday encounters into grumpy tales of the past versus the present, the past being vastly superior... I know it, you know it. It's time for those damn kids to know it. If their parents did a good job raising them, they will thank you for your sage wisdom and realize just how right you are... sadly, don't expect this. With each observation shared, you will leave a lasting impression and become a master of observational grumpiness, educating those fortunate enough to engage in conversation with you.

The Grumpy Dialogue: Forging Connections through Discontent

Grumpy commentary should never be a solitary pursuit. Instead, seek out spirited grumpy dialogues with kindred spirits who appreciate the art of discontent. These encounters become more than just conversations; they are the battlegrounds where grumpy minds clash, inspire, and elevate one another. If you want to be the best, you have to compete with the best, and by compete I mean measure your grumpy yardsticks via grumpy dialogue.

In the realm of grumpy banter, finding a well-matched sparring partner is akin to discovering a rare gem. Together, you embark on a journey of mutual inspiration and challenge, fueling the flames of your grumpiness. In no time, you will create a dynamic synergy that elevates your discontent to new heights. In these dialogues, let your grumpy brilliance shine. Engage in verbal sparring that leaves no stone unturned, no societal absurdity unchallenged, no idiot unmocked. Take turns unleashing your biting wit, exchanging clever remarks and observations that evoke laughter, eye rolls, and nods of agreement. It is within these moments that grumpy camaraderie is born. Through the bond forged in grumpy banter, you will find solace, a shared understanding, and, above all, validation in your grumpy ideals.

Grumpy Targets and Etiquette: Grump Responsibly

In the realm of grumpy commentary, you must take aim with discernment and exercise steadfast restraint when necessary. While our discontent fuels our words, it is crucial to direct your verbal volleys at deserving targets. Choose wisely, focusing on the scenarios that warrant your grumpy input rather than launching indiscriminate attacks on individuals who don't deserve your grumpy wrath.

For example, imagine you find yourself at the supermarket, observing a young bagger learning the ropes. In such a situation, we must exercise understanding and give them a pass for the inevitable mistakes they may make. After all, they are on a journey of growth and should be applauded for their hard work.

However, picture an encounter with an overexuberant youth who mindlessly throws items into your grocery bag, completely oblivious to the delicate nature of your shopping, their earbuds blasting music as they pay no attention to the fact that they just placed a watermelon on top of your precious eggs. In this moment, the stage is set for your grumpy intervention.

It is important to recognize the distinction. Your grumpy commentary should be targeted at those who exhibit acts of carelessness or disregard or the like, rather than those who are genuinely trying their best. It's important to be a grump, not an asshole. Let us reserve our grumpy wrath for those deserving of our discontent, where our words can serve as a catalyst for their inevitable demise. Use well the skills you have learned here, and remember to interject any combination of facial expressions, sighs, and commentary—let it all fly. In order to not seem like a complete lunatic, it's best to start small and build to a resounding crescendo of crotchetiness.

Building Your Grumpy Repertoire

As we approach the culmination of this important journey through grumpy commentary, it is time to focus on building your grumpy repertoire. We shall explore three essential forms of grumpy expression, each with its own unique flavor and purpose. Prepare to expand your grumpy arsenal and leave a lasting impression on the world.

This is by no means an exhaustive list, just a starting point for you to hone your skills.

Form 1: The Quip - The Grumpy Arrow Shot from the Hip

Think of the quip like a verbal arrow shot straight from the hip. It is a quick, sharp retort that catches others off guard with its wit and brevity. Keep your quips at the ready, poised to strike whenever the opportunity arises. The key lies in delivering them with impeccable timing, leaving your target simultaneously amused and slightly wounded. In a matter of seconds, your grumpy quip can leave a lasting impression, evoking laughter and grudging admiration. This is a not a takedown shot but rather a swift and subtle jab. It is a passing quote, comment, or witty remark that leaves the recipient momentarily stunned, unsure of how to respond. As your target reels from the impact of your grumpy arrow, their amusement mixes with a tinge of wounded pride. They may even find themselves chuckling begrudgingly, unable to deny the cleverness of your retort. Job well done.

Form 2: The Grumpy Rant - Unleashing the Floodgates of Frustration

Ah, the grumpy rant, one of life's true indulgences, a glorious release of pent-up frustration that knows no bounds. It's that exhilarating moment when we unleash the floodgates of discontent, giving voice to our grievances with a ferocity that cannot be contained. Let your words surge forth like an unstoppable tempest, obliterating the annoyances of the world and leaving behind a trail of shattered complacency and a sense of relief and vindication.

Let there be no filters or inhibitions. It's your opportunity to express yourself with unadulterated and unapologetic grumpiness. Find the perfect balance between rawness and eloquence, ensuring that every word carries the weight of your discontent. As the floodgates burst open, let your frustrations pour forth with unbridled intensity, tearing down the walls of indifference that surround you.

In the echoes of your words, find liberation and empowerment, knowing that you are not alone in your grumpy perspective. Even if you stand alone in the room, your grumpy rant reverberates with the shared frustrations of fellow grumps through the ages. It's a thunderous chorus of discontent that demands to be heard, and damn the consequences.

Form 3: The Satirical Essay - Dissecting Absurdities with Grumpy Intellect

A playground for grumpy souls to unleash their discontent with the eloquence of a grumpy Shakespeare, Dive into the realm of absurdity and let your pen dance with wicked delight as you expose the follies of society. There's no room for reflection or lofty ideals here—just pure, unadulterated grumpiness expressed through the art of satire.

Summon your inner grumpy bard and weave words with the finesse of a master storyteller. Craft narratives that teeter on the edge of insanity, laced with biting wit and a touch of madness. Embrace the absurdity of life and channel your discontent into scathing observations that leave readers gasping for breath amidst fits of grumpy laughter and pearl clutching alike.

Let your satirical essay be a torrent of grumpy discontent, a tempest of words that shakes the foundations of convention. Spare no one from your razor-sharp quill as you skewer the absurdities that plague our existence. With every stroke, revel in the joy of your grumpy prose, knowing that you are giving voice to the frustrations that dwell within the grumpy corners of your soul.

Grumpy Expressions

Forging Your World-Class Grumpy Legacy

As a grumpy old man, you possess the power to craft a personal legacy of unparalleled grumpiness, a testament to your unique brand of disgruntlement. It is your solemn duty to etch your mark upon the annals of grumpy history, leaving behind a lasting impression for all to behold.

Embrace this noble quest, my brother, and unleash the full force of your grumpy prowess. Cultivate your own voice of grumpy authority, honing your skills with relentless determination. Remember to share your acumen with those who dare to traverse the path of discontent, inspiring them to embrace their own grumpy destinies.

In this journey, observation becomes your ally as you scrutinize the absurdities of the world with a discerning eye. Timing becomes your weapon as you deliver biting remarks and scathing retorts with impeccable precision. Let your discontented spirit soar, unfettered by societal norms, and unleash a torrent of grumpy brilliance upon the world.

By forging your world-class grumpy legacy, you ensure that your mark will be etched in the annals of grumpiness for all eternity. Each grumpy word, each scowl, and each sigh becomes a testament to your unrivaled grumpy greatness. Embrace the power within you and seize the opportunity to leave a cantankerous legacy that will be remembered and revered by future generations. You deserve it.

Continuing Education in Grumpiness

As we conclude this first volume, we have laid the foundation for your transition from middle aged and successful to old and grumpy. We have made huge strides learning the fundamentals and advanced facial expressions, many variations of grumpy sighs and the differences between them, and finished up on grumpy commentary, learning the various ways to communicate your grouchy disposition.

It's still a wide-open world out there, but fear not, for our adventure has only just begun! In the next volume, we shall venture into the enchanting realms of grumpy hobbies and adventures, where we seek solace and joy amidst the chaos of the world.

Until we meet again, may your days be filled with exasperation and your nights with mumbled complaints. Embrace the grumpy journey with unyielding resolve, for together we shall navigate the treacherous waters of grumpiness and emerge victorious, leaving a trail of eye rolls and bemused expressions in our wake. Onward we march, my fellow grump, to new horizons of grumpy enlightenment!

The Grumpy Guidebook

Volume 2
Grumpy Pastimes

Old & Grumpy, LLC
Vincent Fratto and Michael Fayol

Volume 2 Prologue

Welcome back, my fellow curmudgeon, to the continuation of your transition, your journey from middle-aged and successful to old and grumpy. In Volume 1, we mastered the art of grumpy expressions, but there is no time for accolades or to rest on our laurels. Instead, we need to set our sights on our daily pastimes. Sure, we enjoy all our hobbies and activities, or we wouldn't do them. But always remember that with great joy comes great responsibility. Responsibility to always maintain our steadfast grumpy disposition, even in those times filled with joy, happiness, and camaraderie with those we hold most dear. And that right there, my friend, is what separates the men from the boys.

Just like in *Volume 1: Grumpy Expressions*, I will be here for your moral support, voice of reason, and guidance as we navigate through the complicated minefield of Grumpy Pastimes. I call it a "minefield" not because of its dangers or a warning to steer clear but because this is where restraint and personal reflection really make you shine as a grumpy master. Grump too little and no one notices, that's no good. Grump too much and you just look like a pompous bore, which is equally undesirable. By the end of this guide, you will confidently occupy that sweet spot between glorious obnoxiousness and grumpy invisibility.

VOLUME 2
GRUMPY PASTIMES

CHOOSE YOUR HOBBY

CHAPTER 1:
Grumpy Hobbies – Around the House

As we age, our grumpy hobbies become crucial to our daily lives—not merely as activities but as personal sanctuaries. In a world that grows noisier by the day, these hobbies are less pastime and more a survival tactic, a defense against the ceaseless onslaught of fools!

Each corner of our home is a strategic stronghold for these grumpy endeavors. Here, the calm within our walls meets the storm of absurdity beyond. Whether it's retreating to a workshop, nurturing a secret garden, or navigating the high-stakes drama of the backyard BBQ, each activity has its own unique flair of defiance.

To the unrefined, these might seem like peaceful pastimes. Really, peaceful? There's nothing 'peaceful' about a hobby that's one wrong move away from utter chaos. You're out there, hammer in hand, when suddenly it's not just nails you're hitting—it's your thumb. Or you find yourself in your garden, thinking you're growing tomatoes when you suddenly realize you're actually farming grubs and snails! And my personal favorite; you're two beers in standing over a cooling grill when you realize the propane tank is empty—that's when everyone starts asking 'When's dinner?'

Nothing in our world is for the faint at heart. So, grab your work gloves and let's get this started.

Thorns and Scorns: Gardening with a Grudge

Whether you prefer flowers or vegetables, gardening is a great way to really "relax." Sure, flowers are beautiful and smell great, vegetables are tasty and healthy and all that crap, but what a racket this has become! Nowadays, there's every gadget, tool, and organic this or that under the sun. I don't mean to be 'that guy,' but back in our day, gardens grew uphill both ways, and the tulips fought off dandelions on their own without being told, out of sheer respect. I remember my dad spinning tales of his

> **PRO TIP:**
>
> *"I have to water the plants" is a great way to get some alone time.*

Grumpy Pastimes

gardening prowess. All he had to do was scowl at the soil to make the grubs run for the hills, roses would become deer resistant overnight, and the tomatoes would no longer get "too much water," whatever that means. The flowers of today have it too easy, that's the problem.

Well, this isn't a complaint fest (though don't get me started on the cost of dirt these days), this is a learning experience. Every over-watered tomato, blade of crabgrass, and aphid infestation should be used as a tool; a tool to sharpen your grumpy disposition for the better. Let's dig in, shall we (see what I did there)?

First things first, gardening is neither easy nor quick. Don't think that just because you bought a small plant at the nursery or home improvement store that the hard part is done for you—far from it. Plants are spiteful, lazy creatures, and those with pretty flowers are doubly so. And just because you have dirt at home in the ground that is full of grass, weeds, and other various plants, it doesn't mean that it's good enough for the plant you just bought... in fact, it's probably not. Think of a garden like a room full of stubborn toddlers. They need your constant attention, or there is no hope for their survival. Flowers can't feed themselves but want to eat all the time. They live in the dirt, but it has to be the right kind of dirt; you can't just plop them in the ground and expect anything to happen.

> **PRO TIP:**
>
> *Don't ignore the garden, what once was a happy place will turn into a nightmare if unattended.*

Also, just like toddlers, if they are left too close to each other without constant supervision or intervention, they will inevitably start fighting with one another, and you will have to break them up. Also, just like kids, counting loudly to three does nothing but make you more upset that nothing is happening. And don't get me started on "companion planting"—that's just an excuse to buy more plants that won't get along, like trying to force cats and dogs to be friends by locking them in the same room.

In the rare moments when your plants do thrive, don't be foolhardy and expect gratitude. Thats when they become like teenagers, blooming defiantly, and demanding even more from you—more space, more food, more water, and more of your last nerve. And heaven forbid you forget a watering session; the silent treatment you'll get from your plants would put any moody adolescent to shame.

Grumpy Pastimes

But it's not all doom and gloom in the garden. Every now and then, between the backaches and the surprise Hun-led snail invasions, you might just find a moment of peace. A solitary bloom that's decided to grace you with its presence, not out of any fondness for you, mind you, but probably just to prove a point of some kind. That's when you'll know all the grumbling, grumpiness, and months of cursing at the soil was worth it.

Equipped with your most comfortable scowl, this is when it's most important to show these plants who's boss. After all, in the grumpy gardener's world, it's not about the harvest or the blooms; it's about the satisfaction of proving you can out stubborn anything that grows in dirt. And maybe, just maybe, you'll get that one perfect tomato that, despite all the challenges, manages to taste like a small, defiant triumph over nature's nonsense.

GARDEN SHED CONTENTS

ACTUAL USEFUL TOOLS

SEVERAL CRACKED TERRACOTTA POTS
VERMIN RESORT AND SPA

LEANING TOWER OF PLASTIC PLANTERS

UNWANTED RESIDENTS

HOES & HOSE

MOUSE TRAP:
• UNTRIGGERED
• CHEESE STOLEN

BBQ – Salt, Pepper, and Grump to Taste

Before we get into this, we must clarify for our friends in the southern States of the US (especially the great state of Texas), where BBQ means something different than it does to the rest of the English-speaking world. If you are in Texas and ask a neighbor to "come on over for some BBQ" and all you're doing is cooking burgers and hotdogs on the gill outside, they will be sorely disappointed, probably not be your friend anymore, and put their house up for sale. For a Texan, BBQ is large amounts of smoked meat—NOT cooked over an open flame; *very* different. And not just in small quantities either but pounds of it, and all different kinds—beef brisket, turkey breast, beef brisket, whole chicken, beef brisket, sausages, and yes, even beef brisket. What the rest of the world calls "BBQ," they call a cookout. Don't confuse the two if you're in the American South, or there will certainly be some truly grumpy people you will have to deal with. Okay, moving on.

Listen, can you hear it; the seductive sizzle of searing flesh on an open flame—whether animal or plant, how can you go wrong? Well, let me count the ways. But before we look deeper into grilling, please heed this piece of advice: don't, under any circumstances, cozy up your grill against your house. Indeed, a melted slice of cheese atop your juicy patty is a thing of beauty, akin to the Mona Lisa of the BBQ world. However, a melted slice of vinyl siding on your burger is somewhat less than optimal—more like a Picasso-esque disaster.

PRO TIP:

Grill placement is a priority. Close enough to be convenient. Far enough so people leave you alone. Also, don't burn your house down.

Grumpy Pastimes

Let me share a pearl of wisdom I once received from a family member: "No self-respecting man cleans their grill; you're just scraping away the extra flavor." Hmm, a tempting thought, especially for those of us who view cleaning with the same enthusiasm as a cat views a bath. However, after two cookouts, "extra flavor" becomes synonymous with "extra carcinogens," and that storied grill quickly evolves from a prized cooking apparatus to a rusty tetanus hazard. So, yes, you can enjoy respecting yourself all the way to the hardware store as you purchase a new grill every year. Or perhaps consider a novel concept: cleaning your grill. Revolutionary, I know.

> **PRO TIP:**
> *If someone requests a well-done steak, give them the worst cut of meat – they won't know the difference.*

Let's not overlook the grand spectacle that is the act of grilling itself. Picture this: You, the grandmaster of the flame, wielding your spatula like Excalibur, face smudged with soot (there can never be too much fire starter), a look of determined concentration as you preside over your domain of sizzling meats and perhaps the odd veggie kebab (for balance, of course). The grill, your altar; the barbecue, your rite; the ensuing feast, your communion. It's a primal dance, one that stretches back to the dawn of man. When that first genius caveman had the idea to grill a brontosaurus burger on a grate made of rib bones, the BBQ cookout was born!

Grumpy Pastimes

Nowadays, we've evolved from cavemen to sophisticated grumps, but remember, seasoning isn't just a suggestion—it's essential. "Thou shalt not subject thy guests to flavorless fare," states the unwritten grill master's commandment. Whether you're a fan of the classic salt and pepper duo, a rub enthusiast, or someone who views marinating as a form of culinary alchemy, remember: the right seasoning transforms the mundane into the magnificent. It's the difference between a meal that's merely consumed and one that's ravenously devoured amid sounds of muffled satisfaction and the occasional grunt of approval.

Mastering the grill is more than just cooking; it's a rite of passage, cherished and passed down across generations. There's immense pride in arriving at a family cookout and being handed the spatula and a plate of raw meat—you've officially made it! Hold your head high, but not for long. Soon, you'll realize you're cooking for the whole crowd, and by the time you're done, the burgers will resemble hockey pucks, the hotdogs will be shriveled, and the chicken legs may look as if they've sprouted varicose veins from sitting so long.

Grumpy Hobbies – Around the House

GRILLER'S TOOL KIT

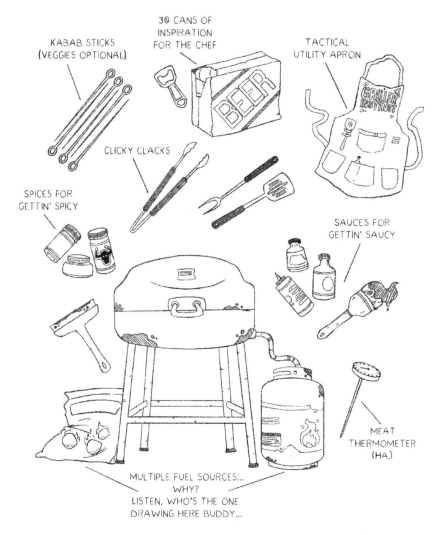

This is the price of culinary command we must pay, though. Fear not, your shoulders can bear the burden, you are strong enough. The silver lining is in knowing that at any time while working the grill, you can just call out "I need a beer," and before you know it, a nice cold one will be in your hand with the top already popped. Enjoy it, brother, you've certainly earned it!

Grumpy Culinary Adventures

...see BBQ...

Home Maintenance with a "Smile"

Drip. Drip. Drip. There it goes again, and, of course, it's two a.m. The faucet couldn't possibly have the decency to start dripping at noon. Water may be the source of life, but in the realm of home maintenance, it's often the bane of our existence. Ignore the well-meaning advice to 'just call the plumber.' Instead, every self-respecting grump has a few tried-and-true techniques up their sleeve. From sternly lecturing the pipes to coaxing them into cooperation and giving a good whack here and there to feel momentarily victorious. It's all about walking that fine line between actually solving the problem and reluctantly admitting that you might just be making things worse.

Grumpy Hobbies – Around the House

SOMETHING BROKE?

HAS YOUR WIFE NOTICED?

- **NO** → DRINK A BEER
- **YES** → YELL AT THE BROKEN THING
  - **DID THAT FIX IT?**
    - **YES** → HOW'D YOU DO THAT?? → TELL EVERYONE YOU KNOW → DRINK A BEER
    - **NO** → HIT IT WITH A WRENCH
      - **DID THAT FIX IT?**
        - **YES** → DRINK A BEER
        - **NO** → CALL A PROFESSIONAL

Maintenance extends beyond the sporadic drips from a faucet or a burnt-out light bulb. The changing of the seasons is nature's way of reminding us that, yes, we have yet more chores to attend to and no, we cannot push them off until next season. Preparing

Grumpy Pastimes

your home for each season should ideally be met with all the enthusiasm of a snail at the starting line of a marathon. But, as a wise man (me) once said; "there is no time like the present to wait until the future." So, let's plan together to go out there and winterize those pipes, rake the leaves, or weed the garden for the umpteenth time—next weekend, or at the very least the end of the game, and then post-game, and then whatever is on after that. Seasonal maintenance is an inescapable reality, my friend; a perpetual struggle that demands our grudging attention, a touch of sophistication, and, let's be honest, a generous amount of procrastination.

TOOL BENCH ESSENTIALS

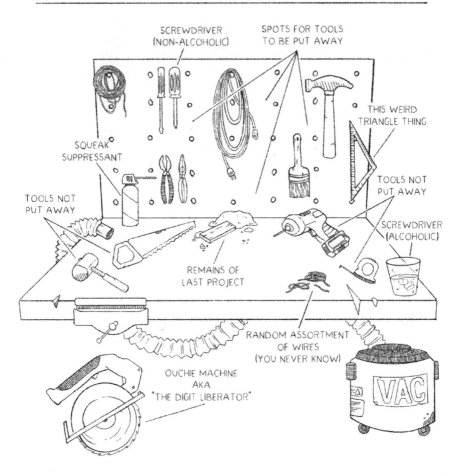

Grumpy Hobbies – Around the House

No matter what you're working on, it starts in your toolshed, garage, or shop, where the air is thick with the musk of oil, sawdust, blood, sweat, and tears. Here, we maintain an essential set of tools not just for their utility but for their ability to endure the inevitable grumbles and gripes of their wielder. From the proudly overused hammer to the #2 screwdriver, a seasoned veteran of the great IKEA assembly war of '09.

> **PRO TIP:**
> *Custom organize your garage, work shed, or tool space so that only you get it. That will help, but not stop, people to stay out of your stuff.*

Like you, I know each tool like the back of my hand, each resilient to the inevitable cursing, smashing of fingers, and flight across the room. These are tools, damn it, not porcelain dolls, they are built to endure. Just don't throw your miter saw or your level (which, amazingly, always seems to be off somehow). You know what, on second thought, maybe it's best not to throw your tools. They're too expensive to replace, and one could even argue that you may hurt someone by throwing a hammer across the room in disgust.

If there is one thing I can teach you here, it's the fine art of letting go, acknowledging that some battles with the home are best left unfought. Learn to coexist with that permanently jammed window, to nod sagely at the mysterious stain on the ceiling that's slowly becoming a feature, and to accept that sometimes, the best way to deal with a problem is to sit down, have a beer, and wait for someone else to notice it. It's not giving up; it's strategic disengagement, with a smile.

The Grumpy Collector: A Curmudgeon's Cache

There's an old saying that everyone says differently but goes something like "keep your hands busy and your mind free." What does that really mean? Heck if I know, but it's a great excuse to start a collection and enjoy some peace, as people tend to leave you alone.

Grumpy Pastimes

The joy of collecting comes from engaging with things you genuinely enjoy. Remember the time when collecting decorative spoons was all the rage? They were pointless to me as a child since I couldn't use them for eating, but my mom certainly enjoyed them somehow.

> **PRO TIP:**
>
> *Collections should be for fun, not a retirement plan. Don't expect baseball cards and collective magnets to take care of retirement.*

As I grew up, it was all about baseball cards and comic books. Today, those old comic books and cards are in boxes collecting dust of their own. These days, though, I've moved on to coins. Partially because coins are always around and are easy to find—heck, they basically come to you! The other side (of the coin) is that they always hold some intrinsic value. Now that's a smart investment, all while being lazy!

The modern collector has evolved beyond the typical spoons, coins, and the like. Many now take pride in assembling and displaying toys and Lego sets. Oddly enough, they aren't unopened boxes but out and put together. Good for them, whatever floats your boat. Keep them busy and out of my hair!

Collecting is twofold. On the one hand, there is the act of actually collecting, and everything that comes along with that, on the other hand, you want to show off your collection! Make sure your treasures are displayed prominently. If someone asks about them, be ready to regale them with tales of your collection for hours. They asked for it, after all!

> **PRO TIP:**
>
> *Feel free to dedicate a room (or two) to showcase your collection! Just tell your significant other I said it was okay to use that room.*

Ultimately, the best part about having a collection is thinking about its future. It's a gift that keeps on giving, leaving your family to wonder, "What the hell are we going to do with all this stuff?" Ah, the joys of a lasting legacy!

Off to a Good Start

These hobbies may disguise themselves as leisurely activities, but for the seasoned grump, they are arenas of quiet conquest, realms where one can exert control in a world that often feels otherwise disordered. They teach us the value of patience, precision, and persistence—qualities that grumps, albeit grudgingly, exhibit in spades. And while these activities might push us to the brink of frustration, they also bring a unique, irreplaceable satisfaction. The kind that only comes from mastering something truly challenging.

As we transition from the stationary pursuits of Chapter 1 to the more physically demanding activities of Chapter 2; prepare to stretch those aching backs and stiff knees. We're about to discover how physical exertion can not only maintain our grumpy demeanor but, surprisingly, also invigorate it. Get ready to tackle the challenges head-on, and, perhaps begrudgingly, admit they might just be enjoyable.

CHAPTER 2:
Grumpy Physical Pursuits

Grumpy Physical Pursuits

Grumpiness can often be like steam building inside a boiling pot, steadily increasing pressure until it finally reaches its boiling point. In this chapter, we'll explore how to channel that pent-up grumpiness into physical activities like golf, pickleball, and more. These seemingly leisurely pursuits may appear innocent enough to the untrained eye, but for the well-versed grump, they are perfect arenas to air grievances, vent frustrations, and flaunt grumpy prowess. So, equip yourself with your clubs, your paddle, or whatever equipment you need, and let's dive into the world of grumpy athleticism, where every swing, every serve, and every step is a chance to unleash your inner discontent.

Grumpy Extreme Sports: Adventures in Avoidance

Extreme Sports, ugh, my back hurts just thinking about this. Alright, let's get it over with. The best way to get through extreme sports when you are as experienced at life as us is to, well… not do them. Climb a mountain? Are you kidding me? Considering it took you twenty minutes to conquer the stairs to bed last

> **PRO TIP:**
>
> *Don't do anything with a friend's kid because they "do it all the time". Translation: they've only done it once or twice at most.*

Grumpy Pastimes

night (at 6:30 p.m., mind you), a literal mountain seems a little too ambitious. Sky diving? First of all, why get into a perfectly good plane just to jump out of it on purpose? And we all know service on airlines is lacking in this day in age, but if you're going to pay for a ticket, you had better make sure they at least land the plane with you inside it. Spelunking? Shoot, I don't even know what that is, but I can tell you with the utmost certainty that you or I have no business spelunking at our age.

Let me encapsulate what we are dealing with here. Just the other night, I returned from a harrowing journey to the kitchen. Sweating and clutching my lower back, my wife sarcastically asked if I was mauled by a bear in there. "No," I 'politely' responded through gritted teeth. My heroic struggle involved peeling an orange and selflessly rescuing a fallen peel from the floor, from which I was able to narrowly escape with my life. A pulled back was a blessing compared to what could have come to pass given that situation. So, let me be as clear as I can be about extreme sports—NO! Just no. A successful and grumpy life is one that needs to be lived with two feet firmly planted on the ground, standing in stark opposition to the ridiculous. Jumping out of planes, climbing mountains and the like are just plain ridiculous.

Poker, Damn Near Killed Her

Behold, the bimonthly poker game—a ritual as ancient as the hills and twice as grumpy. Picture, if you will, a motley crew of curmudgeons gathered around a table, each face lined with a lifetime of grievances, engaged in a silent battle of wills and wagers. With each session, the host's mantle rotates, subjecting each player to the peculiarities and discomforts of their fellow grumps' domains.

The snack situation is a gamble of its own. One session offers nothing but stale pretzels paired with tepid soda; the next, it's organic fruit salad and 'gluten free/non-GMO' water on the menu. Another point of contention is always the lighting, ranging from blindingly bright—like an interrogation room—to frustratingly dim, making it a challenge to even see your cards. And the chairs—oh, the chairs—squeak and rock unevenly with every shift in weight (front left, back right, front left, back right). These pretzels are stale enough, just stick one under the leg and problem solved.

> **PRO TIP:**
>
> *If you bring snacks, don't be cheap and take the snacks home with you at the end of the night.*

Yet, amidst these myriad annoyances, there's an undeniable camaraderie. This shared bond is forged in the fires of mutual grumpiness. After all, the game isn't really about the quality of snacks or the comfort of seating; it's about the thrill of the bluff, the adrenaline rush of a well-played hand, and the sheer joy of outsmarting your friends, if only for a moment. So, embrace the chaos, my grumpy brother, and let the bimonthly poker game stand as a testament to the enduring power of grumpiness in all its glorious forms.

Grumpy Pastimes

Bonding at Bowling

With the pungent smell of lane oil, stale beer, and foot sanitizer, the local bowling alley is the backdrop for our next stop on this crazy journey. All around you the sound of thunder is heard as balls crash into pins. The grunts of victory and the groans of despair linger as someone leaves the dreaded 7 – 10 split behind. Occasionally, you'll hear a sharp "Come on!" as those stubborn 5 pins teeter without dropping along with the rest of their slain kin.

It's impossible to discuss bowling without commenting on the fashion parade on each lane. Every bowler proudly struts their 'stuff' in shoes that were not even in style in the 70s. Sure, I get it, they are utilitarian and serve a specific purpose, but come on now.

In the world of bowling, participants typically fall into one of two categories: The Amateur and the Over-the-Top Semi-Pro-But-Not-Really (who isn't really fooling anyone). Oh, that reminds me, did you know there's a little-known and completely undocumented medical phenomenon related to bowling? Yes, it's true, a curious defect exists in the human brain exclusively linked to bowling prowess. Once a bowler's average score surpasses 110, a miraculous event occurs within the depths of the cranium. This phenomenon involves the 'spare-medial lobe,' a mysterious gland lurking in our brains. When activated by consistent mediocre-to-decent bowling scores, this gland splits wide open, releasing a unique endorphin rush. This not only heightens the bowler's desire to hang out at the lane well before or after their game, but it dangerously lowers their resistance to splurging on excessively expensive bowling gear and garishly patterned shirts. Thus, this fragile lobe is all that stands between a casual bowler and a full-blown bowling fanatic draped in custom shoes, wielding a glittery ball and no less than fifteen unneeded accessories in their bowling bag. It's a sad phenomenon.

> **PRO TIP:**
> *the "spare-medial lobe" isn't real, so don't include it in your medical exams. Stuffy academics frown upon made up facts such as this.*

BOWLING BAG CONTENTS

It's almost too easy to distinguish between the two main species of bowlers; you might as well do it with your eyes closed. Let's take a closer look at each quickly.

Amateurs

These folks show up because they "have nothing better to do" or, worse yet, with a gaggle of kids running around yelling and screaming because their kids have "nothing better to do." You know as soon as they walk in with all those screaming kids, they will be assigned the lane directly next to yours, without fail. Then comes the twenty minutes or so hunt for little Timmy and Sally to find a ball amongst the rows and rows of stock balls that look like they have been there since before the internet.

Grumpy Pastimes

Over-the-Top-Semi-Pro-But-Not-Really Dedicated Bowler

In stark contrast, The Over-the-Top-Semi-Pro-But-Not-Really Dedicated Bowler doesn't simply "show up" at the bowling alley for their league game, they make an entrance in style and at least an hour early. The Best-in-Show even boast about their team's custom shirt that somehow gleams in the dim light of the alley, with their overly stocked bowling bag in hand, ready to take on the world. After a beer or two and a couple bad slices of pizza, of course, it's time for these specimens to don the lane, which can be a spectacle to behold. Custom bowling balls aren't just taken out of the bag, they are carefully extracted like a newborn baby, then gently rocked in a towel and jostled a bit with the utmost care, you know, right before they hurl it down an oiled lane as hard as they can at ten stationary, hard, wooden pins.

The choice between the two is yours, but I warn you to choose your path wisely; for once you embrace one of these roles, there is no turning back. This choice can also affect friendships and relationships. Imagine inviting one of your Amateur friends or non-bowler significant other to your weekly Over-the-Top-Semi-Pro-But-Not-Really bowling nights for a "fun time." By night's end, you might find your circle of friends just a little smaller from one or both sides. Bowling isn't merely a game; it's a full-fledged lifestyle.

> **PRO TIP:**
> *Some people enjoy a bit of "loose juice". This is normally a beer or cocktail to loosen up, so you don't play stiff.*
>
> *BEWARE – being loose advances to sloppy really quick!*

Keep Calm and Golf On

Golf is often called the most relaxing frustrating thing in the world. That statement is a contradiction, you say? Then you clearly have never experienced the joys and agonies of this fun and unique game. The way I see it, there are two types of golfers, not unlike the world of bowling. First, those that suck, like me, but like to play anyway. Then, there are those who, in comparison, might as well be Tiger Woods. These are the players who breeze through eighteen holes at near par, seldom losing a ball.

Grumpy Pastimes

Regardless of skill level, every golfer relies on their trusty set of clubs—typically around a dozen in a full set, each suited for specific distances and scenarios. However, if you're like me, I only use a handful of clubs. I have the "*How the hell am I going to get the ball all the way over there: driver,*" the "*I still have to get the ball all the way over there: iron,*" and we can't forget the "*Seriously, again with the sand?: wedge.*" To round my set off, I carry the "*I'm only three feet away but will take five more strokes: putter.*" Thats my full set, along with a box of balls for every outing. What a game!

With golf, it's important to remember there are some rules and etiquette that are expected to be followed on the course, grumpy or not. If you're playing a round and that pesky foursome of older ladies behind you is constantly waiting for you and your one buddy to finish the hole, it might be time for you two to pull over and have a beer. Let them play through. Feel free to give them an epic "Brow Lift Cataclysm" as that foursome of ladies plays through, though.

> **PRO TIP:**
>
> *What's a "Brow Lift Cataclysm," you ask? Go reread Vol. 1: Grumpy Expressions*

As you navigate the course, remember, even though you're driving a cart, this isn't the time for off-roading. Yes, it's motorized, and yes, you're behind the wheel, but the beautifully manicured greens are not designed for donuts and stunts. If your cart is catching air, you're definitely doing something wrong. And if a couple of beer cans clatter to the ground when you exit the vehicle—no worries, just pick them up. Most importantly, keep that cart on the path!

Gone Fishing

Let's go fishing, the quintessential grumpy pastime where patience is a virtue and catching fish is not only completely optional but commonly not expected. As we prepare to embark on another fishing adventure, let's arm ourselves with our trusty rods, a healthy dose of skepticism, and, of course, our signature scowls.

Grumpy Physical Pursuits

One of the greatest joys of fishing is the opportunity to revel in your grumpy solitude while sitting by the water's edge or floating in a boat. Here, armed with nothing but a pole and your thoughts, you can revel in the peace that only a body of water can provide. Take this time to bask in your grumpy happiness, undisturbed, except perhaps by the occasional fish that dares to disrupt your brooding by biting your bait. It's a time to reflect, to stew over grievances, and to enjoy the quiet, all while half-hoping the fish aren't secretly plotting against you. Because, as any seasoned angler knows, those damn things are cunning and could very well be organizing a resistance against your hook.

PRO TIP:

Keep a collapsable rod and small tackle box in your trunk for impromptu fishing.

Anyone who's anyone who fishes knows all too well there is a ritual to the whole thing. One can't just show up willy nilly at the lake and expect to catch anything. That's when nature gets involved and ruins your outing. That Zeus can really be a jerk sometimes.

Grumpy Pastimes

So, in all seriousness, there is a simple three step ritual, a rite of passage if you are to be successful on the water. This system is fully backed by science, so heed my advice if you want to catch fish. Yes, I said science.

Step 1: Scold the Bait:

Fishing starts with the bait, so before casting your line, take a moment to sternly lecture your bait on its life choices. Remind them of their difficult and noble task of tricking the cunning fish in the depths below. Employ a tone of voice one might use to scold a lazy cat. This step is absolutely vital, don't skimp on the facial expressions here—bait (be it worms or those fancy, shiny lures) really respond to this type of grumpy encouragement.

Grumpy Pastimes

Step 2: Threaten the Gear:

As you prepare to cast, whisper a grumpy threat to your fishing rod and reel. Let them know in no uncertain terms that you expect them to perform flawlessly under threat of being replaced or tossed themselves into the water. This not only sets the stage for the blame game should you catch nothing, but it also imbues your fishing gear with a sense of impending doom, possibly coaxing them into better cooperation. Remember, it's science.

Step 3: Command the Water:

Once you cast your line and are settled in, wag your finger at the water and quietly shout your commands to it and the fish below. For optimal results, tilt your hand at no more than a 43-degree angle to the Southwest with your index finger at the ready, then command the fish to bite, pointing directly at them. Use a firm, authoritative tone with stern eyebrows and a wrinkled forehead. Order them to cooperate, making it clear that you will except nothing less. This not only reinforces your expectations of them but could potentially confuse any pain in the ass eavesdropping fish into compliance and prevent them from conspiring.

> **PRO TIP:**
> *The angle of your wagging hand doesn't really matter.*

Above all, remember to embrace the grumpy spirit, laugh in the face of disappointment, and never let the lack of fish dampen your grumpy resolve. And before I forget, don't be a butthead, take all your empty beer cans and beef jerky bags with you when you go, we aim to be grumpy, not disgusting.

Pickleball: 1 Part Tennis, 2 Parts Vinegar

Pickleball? It sounds like the result of a drunken bet between a tennis player and a ping pong player. "Let's combine the two, but let's add a dash of confusion and call it pickleball!" And just like that, we have a sport that's as ridiculous as it is confusing. And who the heck came up with that name? Makes no sense.

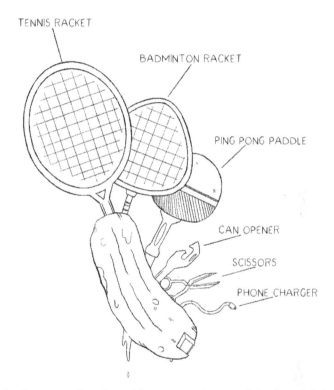

ARTIST'S RENDITION OF WHAT A PICKLEBALL PADDLE/RACKET MIGHT LOOK LIKE

Now, before we dive headfirst into the world of pickleball, let's take a moment to ponder its very existence. What is pickleball, you ask? Well, that's an excellent question—I have no bloody idea. Hold on, let me consult the oracle of our time—the wise and all-knowing Google.

Alright, I'm back. I know that took longer than expected, but I had to hit the restroom, you know how it goes at our age. So, here we are, face to face with the mysterious sport known as pickleball.

Grumpy Pastimes

According to the all-knowing Internet, it's a hybrid of tennis, badminton, and ping pong, played with paddles and a whiffle ball on a miniature tennis court. Sounds simple enough, right? Wrong.

Pickleball is a grumpy person's nightmare disguised as a recreational activity. The paddle is oddly shaped, not quite a tennis racket and not quite a ping pong paddle, and is actually pretty awkward to swing. The court is large enough for a couple of people to play on but not as large as a tennis or racquetball court, so while you have room to move, you don't always feel like you have enough space. Finally, there is the business of pickling the ball (sorry, I just had to go for the low hanging fruit here), it doesn't matter how much calcium chloride you put in the pickling solution, the ball just never stays firm or crunchy.

> **PRO TIP:**
>
> Don't be the "I used to be a tennis player" or worse "I used to always win at backyard badminton"!

This game has become so popular that the inevitable will eventually happen, you will have to step on the court and play this crazy game at some point. But fear not, armed with your paddle and a healthy dose of aggravation, you'll take to the courts and show the world what confusion truly looks like. And if there's one thing we grumps excel at, it's turning confusion into chaos—and maybe, just maybe, having a bit of fun along the way.

CHAPTER 3:
Grumpy Adventures – Embracing Discontented Explorations

Grumpy Pastimes

Here we are, the last chapter in this grumpy guide. Together, we will venture out into the great unknown and try to make it back with a scowl no larger than when we began. Whether you are crammed in a car, 'enjoying' the great outdoors, or trying to retain your sanity in an art gallery, going out is not for the faint of heart or grumpy of soul.

Road Trips, or As I Like to Call Them; 'Hell No'

Road trips are for a group of frat boys, young families, or unsuspecting tourists who haven't yet learned the true meaning of misery on wheels. And you, my friend, like me, are none of those things. Just the thought of spending hours, days, or, God forbid, weeks in a cramped car with anyone but myself sends shivers up my weak, cranky spine. I'll say it again, 'hell no.'

What made the Griswold's trip so hilariously relatable was its uncanny resemblance to the trials and tribulations faced by anyone who has dared to embark on a journey of that magnitude. From the agonizingly long stretches of highway to the inevitable breakdowns

> **PRO TIP:**
>
> *Make sure you know exactly where your significant other's line is, and for the love of all that is holy, don't cross it. Tiptoe that line to a fraction of a micron, but DO NOT go over it.*

and detours, their misadventures struck a chord with anyone who has ever contemplated the merits of staying home instead.

Unfortunately for us, the inevitable always seems to happen, doesn't it? And how can you say "no" to your loved ones when they really have their hearts set on a long family trip? Really, I mean it, how can you say "no?!" I have yet to figure out how to say "no" and make it stick... if you have any insight, please let me know! But I digress, you're going on that trip whether you like it or not. So, you might as well let it be known you don't want to go. This is where all your training as a grumpy master will really pay off. For not only do you not have anywhere to go in that tiny coffin they call a car but neither do your passengers. Let's count the ways we can express our displeasure with the current situation.

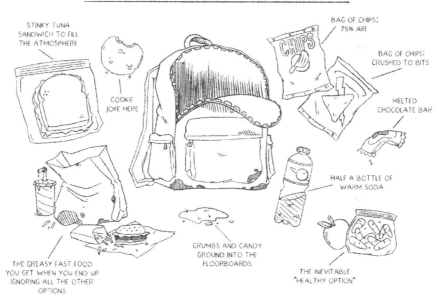

At some point along the way, you will have to stop for gas. Take that time as you're looking for a station to stop at to inform your passengers that gas is way more expensive out here than it is at home.

Grumpy Pastimes

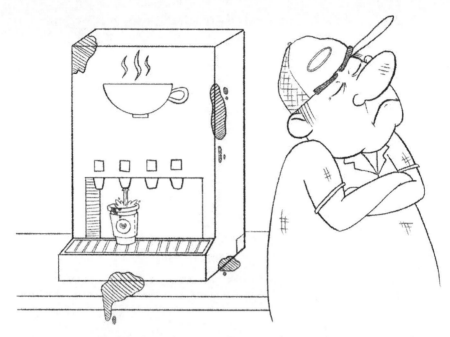

Starting to drag a bit? Sounds like you need a good cup of coffee. This is the perfect time to let everyone know that gas station coffee is either going to be too hot or cold, there isn't enough or there is too much sugar, or my personal favorite *'pfft, my palate is way to finely tuned to accept this subpar bean juice, it's shouldn't even be called coffee. But since we're out here, I'll suffer through it—for you.'* You can forget about finding that 'Goldilocks zone' of coffee out here, you might as well prepare yourself for the colonoscopy in a cup that gas stations call coffee.

After driving for a while, your butt and back will start to ache. Believe you me, you'd be surprised how much discontent you can express with an exaggerated back flex and some deep throated, drawn-out grunts. Shift from one cheek to the other with a sigh that tells your co-pilot you expected the express but got the local, and on top of it all; it's full of traffic and the road is under construction.

We've gotten this far, and now your passengers are fully aware of your displeasure; so, good job, that was tough. But the cruel world just has to hit back, doesn't it—it can't just let you revel in your grumpy happiness. Let's take stock of where we are, hours away from anywhere and just past the 50th mile marker for road construction and poorly placed cones without seeing a single worker! Not that the progress of the work matters to you, you won't be there to enjoy the fruits of that municipality's labor. You just have to suffer through the pothole infested, single lane that's way too tight, and nitwits on the road for hours on end.

> **PRO TIP:**
>
> *Pack ample snacks and drinks, but Beware—don't overdo it without knowing where the next rest stop is!*

So, in short, say it with me, my friend: "Hell No."

The Grumpy Outdoors

I don't know about you, but I've communed enough with nature in my life to last me until the end of time. Have you ever been chased by a bear? Well, fine, I haven't either, but it's certainly not on my bucket list, and I don't think it would be as fun as it sounds. When it comes to camping, I am definitely not looking forward to the joys of sleeping in that burrito bag on a pile of rocks. Not to mention trying to convince myself that the sound outside my tent is just a friendly raccoon and not a hungry mountain lion or a crazed hockey-mask-wearing-psychopath.

But if the day does come when you find yourself surrounded by trees, a small fire, and a tent with skin as thin as a wet sheet of paper, remember my advice and you'll end up just fine, most likely getting out of this alive.

Step 1 - Don't Panic

This is crucial advice, so take it seriously. If you find yourself in the absolute middle of nowhere, likely accompanied by individuals whose decision-making skills are now highly suspect. These people, whom you previously considered friends or even loved ones, have somehow convinced you that abandoning the comforts of modern civilization for the wilderness was a splendid idea. First, take a deep breath—in through the nose, out through the mouth, try to get your heartrate under control. Remember, losing your cool won't help you regain your composure. It's okay. Really, you're going to survive this... probably. Now, with your composure forcibly collected, bravely move on to Step 2.

Step 2 - Panic

Okay, now that we have the helpful "don't panic" drivel out of the way, it's time to do what any other self-respecting grump would do in this situation and panic. Don't get me wrong here, I'm certainly not telling you to throw your hands up in the air and run around like a lunatic with your hair on fire, but let's take stock of the bleak reality: You are surrounded by far too much nature and way too many overly cheerful camping enthusiasts, the situation is ripe for a five-alarm grumpy meltdown. Give in and let the panic wash over you like rain through the leaky tent you're bound to sleep in tonight. As you come down from your fit of panic, it's time to sober up with Step 3.

Grumpy Adventures - Embracing Discontented Explorations

Step 3 - Succumb to Reality

It's time to be honest with yourself with a stark reality check. Here you are, deep in the embrace of nature, which, contrary to popular belief, isn't all that embracing. The fact remains, you're out here now, and yes, it's cold and drizzling. Yes, there is a colony of snakes and spiders patiently waiting for you in your sleeping bag, which is all just part of nature's welcoming committee. And let's not forget, devoid of all modern comforts, your situation is truly grim. But the true cherry on top of this disastrous sundae—Rowan is pulling out the acoustic guitar... ugh, who let Rowan come and why isn't anyone stopping him?!

All this adds up to a terrible time played out to Rowan's soundtrack on repeat and the inevitable subsequent trip to the

Grumpy Pastimes

drug store to buy no less than seventeen different types of ointment. Great, my skin burst out in a rash just thinking of it. Yet, despite this cascade of misfortunes, you've ventured too far to turn back now. You must soldier on and recall the lessons of Step 2. This time, though, really lean into that panic, and forget what I said about not throwing your hands up... this is the appropriate time to do so!

> **PRO TIP:**
> *Don't be a hero, bring quality supplies. You are no longer that boy scout from generations past.*

Oh my God, SHUT UP, ROWAN!

I've Got so Much Culture it's Coming Out My...

Culture? Oh, let me tell you about culture. We're not just steeped in it; we're practically marinating in a rich brew of traditions and pastimes that have nothing to do with silent galleries or echoey opera halls. Our kind of culture is the sort that's been aged to perfection, like a fine wine or an even finer whiskey. Our type of culture is so abundant it's practically spilling over, seeping out of every pore and, dare I say, coming out our rear-end. It's robust, it's hearty, and it's unapologetically ours. It's the kind of culture that doesn't need the validation of a framed certificate or a plaque on the wall. You see, when most people hear the word "culture," their minds drift toward the highbrow, the elite gatherings where everyone nods in agreement over things they don't truly understand, or worse, don't even enjoy.

But not you or me. No, our definition of a cultural evening doesn't involve intermissions or silently pondering the meaning behind abstract splotches on a canvas. Forget the stiff-backed chairs of the opera house, where you're more likely to doze off than decode the dramatics of a foreign language sung at glass-shattering pitches. And poetry forums? They're just not our scene, with their endless metaphors about nature's fury and the human condition recited in dimly lit rooms that smell faintly of desperation and overly expensive, bad coffee.

Give me the real deal any day. The raw, unfiltered joy of cheering for our team at a ball game, the crack of the bat, the roar of the crowd, the taste of victory, or the sting of defeat—it's all part of the

Grumpy Pastimes

rich tapestry of our form of culture. You want culture, I'll hand you a whiskey, aged just right, its warmth spreading through you as a keen reminder of simpler pleasures. And what's more culturally enriching than a smoky cookout? The sizzle of meat on the grill, the laughter of friends and family gathered round, the stories and jokes shared under the open sky. That's the essence of our culture. It's lived, it's loved, and it's anything but quiet and restrained. So, you can keep your silent auctions and your whispered museum tours. We'll be over here, living our culture out loud in the most deliciously "unrefined" way possible. You want culture? I got your culture right here!

> **PRO TIP:**
> *Look into dress code before going, then tweak the look to your style. Going purely without thought makes it awkward. Trust me – I know :(*

However, if you do find yourself inside the walls of an art gallery, whether you chose to be there or not, there are certain ways you can blend in and have some fun at the same time. For example, when faced with an abstract amalgamation of shapes and colors, resist the urge to blurt out, "My kid could do that!" Instead, tilt your head slightly, squint your eyes, and murmur something about the fascinating use of space—and remember the first 'a' in 'fascinating' must be spoken at least two octaves higher than the rest of the word. It's all about blending in, even if inside, you're calculating how many pizza slices the entry fee could have bought you. Come to think of it, forget slices, how many pizza pies you just lost out on.

In the likely event you are standing in earshot of an art enthusiast, those who float from piece to piece, spouting jargon like "postmodern deconstruction" and "neo-expressionist revival," It's crucial in these moments to nod along as though you grasp the gravity of their commentary, resisting the temptation to ask if they even know what that means. Remember, the goal here is to emerge from the gallery unscathed and with your sanity intact by exuding an aura of faux appreciation. After all, art is subjective, and today, you're a master of disguise, navigating the gallery with the grace of someone who's lost but too proud to ask for directions.

Call of the Live Show

While this book champions the grumpy lifestyle, let's not forget the importance of enjoying ourselves every now and then. Whether it's a solo outing to clear your head or a group excursion to share some laughs, live entertainment offers something for everyone. From comedians to theater productions or your favorite bands, this is your time to savor the pleasures of the arts.

Relaxing with a drink in hand, especially while indulging in your favorite performances, can be incredibly satisfying. Go alone if you like; this is your opportunity to have a good time without worrying about anyone else's experience. Who cares if someone else is having fun? This moment is for you to connect deeply with music that resonates or comedy that pushes boundaries—enjoying what you love in your own way.

Grumpy Pastimes

However, sharing these outings and experiences can also bring people together like nothing else. That's why we flock to massive music festivals and pack theaters. So, occasionally, it's worth bringing friends or family along for the ride, as long as they agree to your terms. And if you have young ones who haven't yet learned what "real music is" or you think they're "too sensitive" and can benefit from a good laugh, bring them along. It's a chance to broaden their horizons, teach them it's okay to let go and see the lighter side of life's absurdities, and show them there's more to music than their playlist. This is about more than just entertainment; it's about expanding minds and opening hearts to new experiences—ones you have already vetted and approved. They will thank you for it!

> **PRO TIP:**
>
> *Heckling tip: Leave the personal stuff at home. The game is heckling, not being a $!@#*

Without even realizing it, due to the varied nature of things you bring them to, you'll be making core impressions on these youth that will help mold them into better people... or at least more fun to talk to.

Lights, Cameria, Grump

Who doesn't like a good movie or the movie theater experience? The large screen with high-quality forty-two speaker sound system and the delicious aroma of freshly popped buttery popcorn. Whether it's an adrenaline-pumping action flick, a thought-provoking drama, or a classic comedy, a great movie provides the perfect escape for an evening. Yet even this escape isn't without its pitfalls.

Consider the cost of concessions: two of the cheapest substances on Earth are corn and soda. So, why, really, why should I have to take out a second mortgage on my house to buy a large popcorn and large soda? I'm not telling you to skip the popcorn and soda, by all means, they will enhance the movie-going experience for sure, but you know going in what it's going to cost. If you don't want to spend the money, don't get it. This might be a guide on how to be a better grump, but as with anything in life; we must always consider the correct time and place. The teenager behind the counter has nothing to do with the pricing and can't do anything about it, so keep those comments to yourself. All you are going to do is ruin their day, and that's not what we are about. So, buy your snack—or don't—and move on.

Grumpy Pastimes

Once settled in your seat, there will inevitably be that one rude person who has apparently never been to a movie theater before and doesn't know the "shut up" rule. This person seems to believe the entire audience is eager to hear their wildly inaccurate plot predictions. Even though it's always completely wrong. I am here to tell you, there are a number of ways that we can work to combat this ridiculousness.

> **PRO TIP:**
> *The best way to battle the rude people is by being where they aren't – the early bird matinee on a weekday!*

This situation is the perfect time and place to unleash "The Sarcastic Arch of Condemnation" stare you learned in Volume 1 of this series. When timed right, this stern look can silence the chattiest of movie-goers and send a shockwave reverberating throughout the theater, scaring off any other would-be offenders. It's about conveying a message that's louder than their whispers: respect the silence or face the wrath of a grump scorned. This does, however, only work if the commentator is sitting behind you. Otherwise, you're just wasting a good quality glare at the back of someone's head, and while it might make you feel a little better about yourself, it certainly won't do anything to quiet the theater's villain.

In the off chance the glare doesn't work, or they are not seated in eyeshot of you, there is always the aggressive 'shush.' It should be sharp, commanding, yet not so loud as to become the very disruption you're trying to snuff out. The key is in its suddenness, a verbal slap that snaps the offender out of their rudeness. Don't let it linger though, it should reach its crescendo quickly and then fade out for maximum effectiveness.

With these tried-and-true tactics employed, you should be able to enjoy the rest of the movie in peace with your gold-plated popcorn and ultra rare cola (at least that's what their prices suggest).

Signing off with a sigh

As we close the curtains on this grumpy guide, let's take a moment to acknowledge the profound irony of this entire endeavor. Yes, we've journeyed together through the insane worlds of extreme sports, road trips, and the great outdoors—only to confirm what we grumps have known all along: every silver lining has a cloud, and it's probably raining.

In *Volume 1: Grumpy Expressions*, we've armed ourselves with stern glares, mastered sighs as profound as War and Peace, and laid the foundation for our grumpy happiness. Here in *Volume 2: Grumpy Pastimes,* we've applied our learnings and delved deeper into our own little slice of the world and came out the other side with an unrelenting scowl. Reenforcing that grumpiness is not just a mood—it's a survival tactic.

If there's one thing to take away from our adventures together, it's that sometimes, the best way to enjoy life is to complain about it just enough to make it bearable—and, occasionally, secretly delightful. So, as you return to your undoubtedly uncomfortable chair to muse over your next grumpy outing, remember that being a curmudgeon isn't about being miserable; it's about loving to hate and hating to love the absurd circus that is life.

Thank you for joining me in this paradoxical parade of pessimism and pleasure. May your days be mildly annoying, your discomforts manageable, and your spirits—like your drink—always half full (or is it half empty?). Here's to many more grumpy adventures together, because, as we've learned, if we're going to be dragged out to experience life, we might as well complain about it.

Fare thee well, my friend. For now.

About The Authors

Vincent Fratto, born in 1978, started his career as a video game artist, then transitioned to the advertising space in 2008. Vincent moved to New Braunfels, Texas in 2021 with his wife and two kids.

Michael Fayol, born in 1978, has worked in the video game industry for the majority of his professional life. He moved to Frisco, Texas after leaving New York in 2016 and just recently moved to the area known as the Austin/San Antonio corridor.

Ian Chamberlin, born in 1991, went to school in Florida studying art and design. After college, Ian moved to New York where he worked with Vinny at the same marketing company, and other various projects over the years leading up to the grumpy guidebook.

Vincent and Michael have been friends since high school and started their professional lives working for the same gaming company, and even played on the same softball team for twelve years. Both originally from the Hudson Valley area of New York state, they have met up again professionally in Texas where they wrote *The Grumpy Guidebook* series as their first authored projects with Ian as the illustrator.

The Grumpy Crew has much more on the horizon as we are working hard every day to write and produce unique books for years to come!

Sincerely,

Vinny, Mike & Ian

Follow For More Grumpy Content

Follow us on our socials for more grumpy content and stay in the know about future books.

Scan Below to Leave a Review

As independent authors not working or publishing through a Publishing House, your review and feedback means so much to us and helps us grow in more ways than you can know!

Printed in Great Britain
by Amazon

5597364e-b78b-4fd5-87da-be348ea5694eR01